Giving Thanks with Halmoni: Celebrating Chuseok,
the Korean Harvest Festival
Text copyright © 2025 Kathleen Choi & Sook Nyul Choi
Illustrations copyright © 2025 Il Sung Na

Published in 2025 by Red Comet Press, LLC, Brooklyn

Library of Congress Control Number: 2024948445

ISBN (HB): 978-1-63655-161-6
ISBN (EBOOK): 978-1-63655-162-3

25 26 27 28 29 TLF 10 9 8 7 6 5 4 3 2 1

First Edition
Manufactured in China
Red Comet Press is distributed by ABRAMS, New York

RedCometPress.com

Kathleen Choi & Sook Nyul Choi   Il Sung Na

GiVING THANKS
WiTH HALMONi

Celebrating Chuseok,
the Korean Harvest Festival

RED COMET PRESS · BROOKLYN

Halmoni stared at the moon lighting the night sky.

"Your grandmother really loves the moon," said Maddy as she too gazed up at the sky.

"The moon is my grandmother's calendar," explained Su-Jin.

"Halmoni still follows the lunar calendar like she did when she was growing up in Korea. Instead of talking about months, she talks about the number of moons. Halmoni said that for centuries that is how the farmers and everyone in Korea kept track of time."

"It's a full moon tonight, right, Halmoni?" Su-Jin asked her grandmother.

"Yes, so perfectly round and bright. The next full moon will be the harvest moon—even bigger and brighter than tonight. It will be Chuseok, the autumn celebration in Korea," Halmoni replied.

"What's Chuseok?" asked Keisha.

"It's the biggest holiday of the year in Korea. Families gather together, show gratitude, remember our ancestors, and share a big feast," Halmoni replied.

"Oh, that sounds a lot like Thanksgiving," said Keisha.

"Yes, I think it is like Thanksgiving," replied Halmoni. "And this year, I will celebrate my first Thanksgiving here with you all.

"I will have turkey and taste Su-Jin's famous cranberry sauce," Halmoni said with a gentle smile.

But later, Su-Jin confided in her friends,
"I'm afraid Halmoni will be sad to miss Chuseok.
She only moved here recently, and I think she
misses Korea and all her family and friends.

"She always hosted the Chuseok dinner for
our family in Korea. I hear my cousins calling
her and asking her for her recipes. I think they
are all really missing one another."

"Why don't we surprise Halmoni with a Chuseok party?"
said Keisha.

"That's a great idea, except I don't even know what you do for
Chuseok," said Su-Jin. "I've heard Halmoni and my cousins from
Korea talk about it, but I've never really celebrated it."

"You said your grandmother was a teacher, right? Could we ask her to teach us how to celebrate Chuseok? Maybe Halmoni can help us throw a Chuseok party for our friends so everyone can learn about it," said Maddy.

"That's a great idea! Halmoni loves teaching us things, and she loves cooking and seeing everyone enjoy her food," said Su-Jin.

"And we can all help!" said Keisha.

The next day, they told Halmoni their idea for a Chuseok party.

"Really? You really think your friends would be interested?" Halmoni replied shyly.

"It will be so fun! You teach us what to make, and we will help do all the work," the girls chimed in cheerfully.

Each evening, as they watched the moon grow smaller and smaller, the girls worked to prepare the little presents that are given out at Chuseok. Halmoni showed them how to wrap things the Korean way—using pretty cloth called bojagi.

"Oh, Halmoni, how pretty you make them!
This one looks like an envelope!" said Maddy.

"And this one looks like a rose!" said Su-Jin.

"And you can reuse these—so this is good for
the environment!" said Keisha.

"I'm going to wrap birthday presents like this
from now on!" added Maddy.

Finally, there was no moon in the sky—only a few stars shining above the city lights. "Now, the serious preparations must begin!" Halmoni exclaimed with excitement.

The next night they spotted a tiny sliver of the moon; each night after that, they watched the moon grow and grow and grow.

The girls helped Halmoni shop for food and make all the traditional foods. Halmoni taught them to make Korean scallion pancakes called pajun, japchae noodles, a traditional beef stew called galbijjim, and three-color vegetables.

"An important part of Chuseok is remembering our ancestors and expressing gratitude to them," said Halmoni.

"Maybe at dinner we can each share what we are thankful for—like my family does at Thanksgiving," said Maddy.

"And maybe I can bring pictures of my great-grandparents to show everyone and tell their stories," said Keisha.

"Those are wonderful ways to celebrate the spirit of Chuseok," said Halmoni.

The night before, when the moon was almost full, they sat around the table to make the very special rice cakes shaped like half-moons called songpyeon. Halmoni showed the girls how to roll out the rice flour dough and stuff them with sweet fillings made of sesame seeds, honey, chestnuts, or sweet red bean paste.

"Oops! This one is a very chubby one! It looks bigger than a half-moon!" said Keisha.

SESAME OIL

BROWN SUGAR

Then they steamed all the rice cakes on a bed of pine needles, filling the house with the scent of autumn.

RICE FLOUR

½ CUP WET RICE FLOUR

BOILED WATER

Finally, it was the day of Chuseok!
The full moon seemed larger and
brighter than ever, the girls noticed.
"Yes," explained Halmoni. "On
Chuseok, the moon lights the sky
from dusk to dawn and it does feel
brighter and bigger than ever.

"The farmers were always happy to have so much moonlight to finish their work by. That is why we celebrate this harvest moon."

Halmoni and the girls set the large feast out on the table and placed a present wrapped in bojagi at each place.

All their friends arrived, and Su-Jin, Maddy, and Keisha greeted each one saying, "Chuseok jal bonaeseyo!" meaning "Have a good Chuseok!"

Everyone loved trying all the special foods, and they shared pictures and stories about their ancestors.

Halmoni showed her parents' wedding picture, and everyone started to laugh.

"Su-Jin, your great-grandmother has one dimple just like you!"

Halmoni then taught everyone how to play Hwatu and Yut Nori—traditional card and board games.

Halmoni smiled as the room was filled
with the familiar slap of the Hwatu cards.

"Happy Chuseok," Halmoni said giving the three girls a squeeze. "I am so thankful for you making me feel so welcome here. And I am so happy you and your friends are interested in learning about other lands and traditions. I can't wait to celebrate Thanksgiving with you and learn from you!"

"At Thanksgiving, we will get to be *your* teachers, Halmoni!"
Maddy, Keisha, and Su-Jin replied in unison. "Happy Chuseok!"
the girls cheered as they joined hands with Halmoni and stared
out at the harvest moon shining so brightly upon them.

What is Chuseok?

Chuseok 추석 is Korea's mid-Autumn celebration that takes place on the fifteenth day of the eighth month of the lunar calendar. It is one of the biggest holidays of the year in Korea. People travel from all over to get together with their families, remember their ancestors, and share a big feast.

Who is Halmoni?

Halmoni 할머니 is the Korean word for grandmother and is also commonly used to refer to an elderly woman.

Can the moon be your calendar?

Used for thousands of years across many different cultures, the lunar calendar is a calendar based on the cycles of the moon around the earth. Today, the calendar most commonly used around the world is called the Gregorian calendar; it is a solar calendar based on the movement of the earth around the sun. Koreans now use the Gregorian calendar, but many Koreans still continue to follow the lunar calendar in addition.

Why do Koreans celebrate Chuseok?

For thousands of years, Korea was an agrarian society of farmers cultivating the land to grow their food. Farming was always very difficult work in Korea, especially because around seventy percent of Korea is made up of mountains! Farmers had to pay close attention to the weather and the seasons; watching the moon was their way of keeping track of the passage of time—the moon was their calendar. For them, the best night of all was the full moon in the eighth month of the lunar calendar which always rose very quickly after sunset and provided early evening light that allowed the farmers to continue their harvesting work. Afterward, they could be outside and rejoice in the moonlight together. While most Koreans these days are not farmers, Chuseok remains one of the biggest holidays of the year. It is a time to remember Korea's agrarian roots and celebrate family, food, and togetherness, and to give thanks to those who came before us.